# BATMAN
## Murder at
## WAYNE MANOR

WRITTEN BY
**DUANE SWIERCZYNSKI**

ILLUSTRATED BY
**DAVID LAPHAM**

COLORING BY
**DOM RAMOS**

Batman created by
Bob Kane

QUIRK BOOKS
PHILADELPHIA

*For my father, who first*
*introduced me to Batman and taught me*
*how to play his theme song.*

Library of Congress Cataloging in Publication Number: 200794224

ISBN: 978-1-59474-237-8
Printed in China
Typeset in Bembo and Chevron

**Designed by Doogie Horner**

Photos on page 31 courtesy iStockphoto

Distributed in North America by Chronicle Books
680 Second Street
San Francisco, CA  94107

10  9  8  7  6  5  4  3  2  1

Quirk Books
215 Church Street
Philadelphia, PA  19106
www.quirkbooks.com

"Man is least himself when he talks in his own person. Give him a mask, and he will tell you the truth."

—*Oscar Wilde*

# THE PLUNGE

My mask is meant to scare.

There is some protection built in, of course. When someone throws a punch at my head, the mask and cowl are designed to redistribute the energy around my head, away from a single spot that could shatter skull or rupture a cranial artery. The mask is also equipped with communication gear and visual enhancements—including night vision.

But mostly, it's meant to scare.

The eyes are sunken. The ears, otherworldly. The molded shape of the skull, exaggerated. No human being looks like this. If there were humans like this, they were weeded out long ago—burned at the stake, erased from evolution. There's a word for humans who look like this: *monsters*.

The only recognizably human part of me under my cowl is my mouth. But even that is meant to frighten. I can bare my teeth and growl, and I reduce the human to the animal.

I want them to think: *This thing can bite*. I want them to know: *I am a hunter of predators. If you prey on the innocent, I will find you and hurt you*. I want them to be scared.

Last night, though, I went too far. It was a stupid mistake—a rookie mistake. Even after more than a year of this, I'm still coming up short.

I was too hard on a guy on a rooftop. He was a sniper, new to town. He was fresh on a contract from a splinter group of the Falcone crime family, and he was notorious for being a bit sloppy. I read up on him. Back in Philadelphia, he had a knack for collateral damage. Too many innocent people were getting clipped on gigs: a grandmother of five; a newly-married man; a nurse coming off the late shift. So the Philly guys sold off his contract to the Falcones in Gotham.

Lucky us.

He was lining up a shot high above Grand Street when I finally caught up with him. I had to take him out. Quickly.

My appearance was meant to scare him, not make him think he was about to be butchered

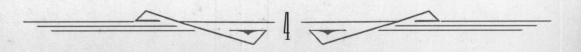

in cold blood. But that's what he thought. He lashed out with the adrenaline-fueled strength of a man who is convinced he is about to die. He thrashed and kicked and yelled and managed to knock me off balance—right off the edge of the roof.

Grand Avenue came speeding toward me. I didn't have my Batrope—the one that's strong enough to support my weight and yet forgiving enough to keep my arms in their proper sockets. I'd used the Batrope to climb up to the roof. The sniper had spotted me before I had a chance to recover the rope, which was now hanging down the other side of the building. It was utterly useless to me.

It's not easy to improvise when you're falling 9.8 meters per second. I have a cape, but the one that's usually attached to my Batsuit is for show only. It's meant to disguise my shape and form—not help me hang-glide over the streets of Gotham.

I saw a blur of windows and lights and then, down below, three wires. I prayed my insulated gloves were enough to protect me, just in case the wires carried live current. I grabbed the outermost wire and pulled it down with me until it snapped in two. I quickly wrapped the torn end around my glove and swung down until my body smashed against the side of the concrete building. The wire tightened so fiercely around my hand I thought it would slice through my fingers. The window shattered to pieces beneath my shoulder. Someone screamed. I twisted around until I was able to look inside. A woman. Working late, papers tumbling out of her arms. I mouthed an apology, then I started the long climb up to another open window.

Then I pounded up the fire stairs.

I hit the roof.

But by then my sniper was gone, and his rifle with him.

I spent the next five hours scouring the city rooftops for any sign of the gunman, or any hint of his target. I came up empty. I must have spooked him hard. As the sun broke over the Gotham skyline, I called it quits. It was a mixed outcome; a killer was still at large, but no one was hit by a sniper's bullet that night.

I returned home to Wayne Manor for a few hours of sleep.

Sleep has been an uneasy state for me during the past thirteen months. The most recent

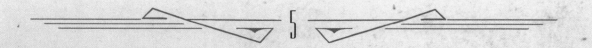

IT'S NOT EASY TO IMPROVISE WHEN YOU'RE
FALLING 9.8 METERS PER SECOND.

events of any given night play out in my dreams, as if my brain cannot accept defeat, as if it intends to roll the footage on an endless loop until it figures things out.

My hand, outstretched, hoping to connect with that wire . . .

My hand, outstretched, hoping to connect . . .

My hand, outstretched, hoping . . .

"Hey, Matty!"

Someone was yelling.

It was a gruff voice, out in the distance.

I rolled over and was mildly surprised to find myself in bed. Immediately I felt how much I had strained my arms the night before. My muscles screamed. It hurt just to push myself up from the mattress.

Oh, Alfred's going to have a field day with this one. Later I would ask for painkillers—the blue ones, extra-strength. He'd insist on giving me a cup of chicken soup and a piece of toast with marmalade on it. Better for you, Master Bruce, he'd say. No one knows this fact about Alfred Pennyworth: he's a sadist.

"Matty, you better take a look at this! Like, *now!*"

Up on my feet, it hurt to pull my bedroom curtains aside. Outside, on the grounds of Wayne Manor, the workmen were finishing up their last day of landscaping. That, too, was my fault. I set up shop in the Batcave about ten months ago before realizing that it needed to be expanded—especially if I wanted to develop forms of transportation other than an armored black car that could run at 160 mph. I decided to do the excavation myself—well, myself and Alfred, and a dozen crates of construction-grade explosives.

A little too much TNT led to a crack in the lawn above the Batcave, which had to be repaired and re-landscaped. Money wasn't the issue. The problem was keeping the construction crew in the dark about what lay below their dirt-caked boots.

That's what worried me right now. Maybe the gap had widened, and there were now a bunch of curious guys in overalls looking down into the Batcave. I imagined the reactions. "Yo, look at that. Is that a black car with a bat on it?"

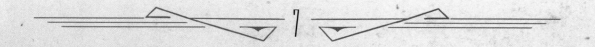

*God, no.*

I wrapped a robe around my body, slid my feet into slippers, quickly checked the full-length mirror to make sure I had no visible cuts or bruises, and then I rushed downstairs. Along the way, I stepped into character: Bruce Wayne, hungover playboy, annoyed by the blue-collar stiffs making too much noise outside.

But, in truth, I was Bruce Wayne, the bruised orphan who was absolutely panicked that the blue-collar stiffs had discovered that he dresses up in a black batsuit and wages a nightly war against the criminal element of Gotham City.

Alfred was waiting for me at the bottom of the staircase.

"A bit early for you, isn't it, Master Bruce?"

The grandfather clock in the foyer said it was 4 P.M.

"I didn't want to miss breakfast," I said. "What's going on outside?"

"I was about to find out."

"Let's go."

We walked across the front grounds. It was a humid summer afternoon. The scent of freshly churned dirt hung in the air.

By the time we made it to the scene, three workmen were watching two others pull something out of the earth that looked like a rolled-up carpet. Something wrapped in a flimsy plastic tarp. It looked old, muddy, and tattered in places.

"Holy blessed mother," one of the workmen gasped. "I think it's a . . . "

He didn't have to finish. Everyone knew what it was.

A dead body.

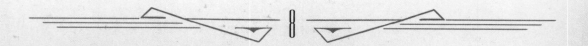

# THE DISCOVERY

Everyone stared at the body, numb with shock.

Or rather, everyone stared at the remnants of a body. It had been human being once, but now it was reduced to a skeleton. Bunches of ripped, dirty plastic were swaddled around the skeletal torso and legs. Instead of being buried in a coffin, this person had been discarded like a bundle of trash.

"So what do we do?" a workman finally asked me.

I recognized him: Matt Foster, the job's foreman. He'd introduced himself the first day on the job, two weeks ago. Hoping to impress the billionaire, I thought at the time. But since then, he'd worked quietly and efficiently. Alfred kept tabs on Matt and his crew; he made a point of noting with amazement that some people were able to leave their work at work. I told Alfred that his point was taken.

Alfred was now shaking his head. His lips were moving slightly—perhaps in prayer.

"I guess we have to call the police," I said, looking at him.

He nodded, then motioned to the body in the tarp and raised his eyebrows.

I'd noticed it too.

The silver mask, clearly a woman's, wrapped around the eyeholes of the skull. It was like someone's sick idea of a joke.

"Who put that on?"

"Nobody, sir," said Foster. "That's how we found her. Swear to God."

"If I find out otherwise, you'll never work in Gotham again."

"Sir, honestly. Nobody touched a thing."

While we waited for the Gotham City PD, I studied the remains. How long had the body been here? It wasn't far from the hole.

That hole.

It was the hole that had frightened me all those years ago.

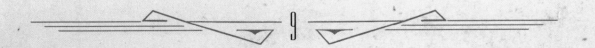

INSTEAD OF BEING BURIED IN A COFFIN, THIS PERSON
HAD BEEN DISCARDED LIKE A BUNDLE OF TRASH.

I was no older than three when I first learned about death. It's funny how fathers teach their sons the important things in life. Mothers try to protect; fathers try to serve it straight.

That was the way of my father, Dr. Thomas Wayne.

I had been stumbling around after my father, who was taking a post-dinner stroll with me. I'd ventured too close to a hole in the ground. One minute it was all summer breezes and sunlight and terra firma, the next I felt my little foot step into nothing. Raw fear raced up my nerve endings. Even though I couldn't see it, I could sense it: Below me was a drop I didn't want to take.

Then I felt my father's hand on my chest, saving me from the fall.

"Be mindful," said Dr. Thomas Wayne, "or there will be no more Bruce."

It was the way he said it—*no more Bruce*—that made it click. Until then, the world was defined as something that surrounded me, enveloped me, cared for me. Then, for the first time, I understood that it could go on without me. Something horrible could happen, and I would be no more.

No more Bruce. That was death.

I wasn't always mindful. A few years later I tumbled down that same hole, chasing a ball across the front lawn. I've written about that experience—the darkness, the bats, and the true meaning of fear—elsewhere in this journal. That tumble into the earth was pivotal to my mission.

But I hadn't thought about those earlier words from my father—*no more Bruce*—until the moment I stood on the front lawn and looked at the dead woman.

*Who are you?*

*Who were you?*

Detective Jim Gordon arrived fairly quickly. This is, after all, Wayne Manor. And his first action in his new cold case investigation was to promptly ask me to vacate the premises.

"Afternoon, Mr. Wayne," he said. "Would you mind waiting inside while the boys and I get started here?"

"This is my lawn, detective."

"And your lawn is now a crime scene. We can't have you compromising anything."

That's when I saw it: a card on the lawn, near the body. It had fallen out of the plastic.

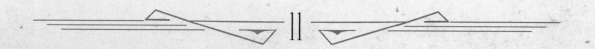

I needed that card.

"Compromising," I mocked, and I started to walk away in a fake huff. I stopped abruptly, turned on my heels, and marched back to Gordon. "I'll let you know if I plan on fleeing the country, Detective."

"Just be reachable by phone," he replied.

I raised a hand at him, dismissively, and turned to walk away again.

That's when I conveniently tripped.

My palms hit the lawn. I heard stifled laughter from the workmen. I clamored back to my feet, pretended to be outraged and embarrassed at the same time, and stormed away. But I had the card in my hand.

Once I was back inside Wayne Manor, I examined it very closely.

"Come on, Alfred. Spit it out."

"Master Bruce, I think it's best if first I . . . "

"Alfred!"

He looked at me sadly. "I'm afraid I recognize that necklace. The woman who wore it worked for your father at Wayne Enterprises, many years ago. But that can't be . . . "

*My father.*

That was all I needed to hear.

Once upon a time, a boy made a promise to his dead parents. *A promise he always keeps.*

# THE SHOCK

Some cities are beautiful at night.

Gotham isn't one of them.

The neon sprawl and shadowy architecture can fool you, if you squint, or if you have had too much to drink. But this city has been overdeveloped and undermaintained; too many grand buildings have been left to fall to ruin.

I drove through the streets, trying not to look at the decay. Every corner was a potential memory trap. Every time I saw the shuttered storefront that used to be a florist shop, I remembered holding my mother's hand when she took me there. She didn't need to shop. Fresh flowers were delivered to the Wayne Manor and arranged daily by our housekeepers. But Mom liked to take me out anyway. She didn't want me to grow up too sheltered.

I saw the bouquets of roses.

I saw my mother's smile.

I felt the ache of her absence.

So as the Batmobile sped through the streets of the city, I tried to keep my eyes dead ahead,

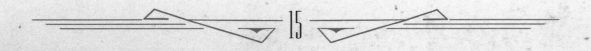

avoiding the memory traps. But it was difficult. I associated too much of the city with my parents. They still believed in Gotham, even when everyone else gave up.

I still believe in it.

I caught Gordon just as he was leaving police headquarters. Knowing the detective, he was darting home for a quick dinner break with Barbara and the kids. Then he would return to headquarters and resume work on the cold case that had dropped into his lap this afternoon.

Gordon wasn't a workaholic, but he had a conscience. He couldn't let the dead lie unspoken for.

He walked right past me, oblivious to the fact that I was perched just a few feet above him, on the roof of the parking lot's guard booth.

"Heard you found a dead girl at the Wayne place today."

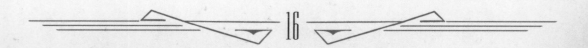

Gordon jolted, dropped his car keys, then cursed. "I hate when you do that."

I grunted. "Rich boy party too hard?"

"No, no," Gordon said, clutching his chest while pretending to smooth out his tie. "It's not like that. The woman appears to have been dead for quite some time. She's nothing but bones. In fact, our guy thinks she's been gone at least thirty years." The detective shook his head.

"Something wrong?" I asked.

"So far, things are pointing to the last person on earth I thought capable of such a crime."

"Who?"

He stared at me. "Our usual deal, right?"

"You know I'm discreet, Detective Gordon."

"Okay. It's looking an awful lot like Dr. Thomas Wayne. Don't know if you know that name. He's Bruce Wayne's father."

In my short war against crime, I've absorbed innumerable punches and kicks. None of them hit as hard as Gordon's words.

"Late father," he added.

I had to be careful not to react. Jim Gordon had no idea who the Batman is, nor did I want him to know. Alfred would sooner die than reveal my identity, and he knows what he's signed on for. But not Gordon. It's best not to put a man with a young family in that sort of position. A man with a family is the most vulnerable of all.

But as I crouched there in the shadows, just a few feet above Gordon's head, I was feeling vulnerable, too.

I thought you couldn't hurt someone who had lost everything he loved. Whose family was already dead.

I was wrong.

"What kind of evidence do you have?" I asked.

"Some tips since the news of the discovery broke," he said. "Not to mention where we found the body."

"Tips? Already?"

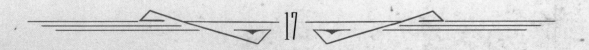

"Phone's been off the hook. The *Globe* guy showed up within minutes. Radio's on it now, too. I've pleaded 'No comment' 47 times in the last half hour."

A member of the construction crew, maybe. Looking to score a bit of extra cash now that the landscaping job was on hold. *Yo, you wanna hear something about a dead body over at the Wayne place?*

"Anything hard?"

Gordon handed me a piece of paper.

"Officially, I didn't give this to you," he said. "But you're good at spotting the odd detail nobody else seems to catch. Maybe you'll find something."

It was a Gotham City PD autopsy report, fresh from the coroner's office. Someone had fast-tracked it. Unusual for a cold case, especially in a city where dead bodies drop on a daily basis. Despite over a year of my war on crime, Gotham City still had the fastest-growing murder rate in the country, outpacing even Detroit and Philadelphia.

"I'll take a look," I told Gordon.

Who was that woman in the ground, Dad? Did you steal her life the way yours was stolen?

*No. It was not possible.*

I decided I would prove it.

# THE MASK

A voice in the alley pulled me away from the memories and the ghosts and the blood.

"You lost, Mr. Wayne?"

The voice was deep, modified somehow—either by a device or vocal training. I knew that when I turned, what I faced would not be friendly.

I turned.

A tall figure stood at the opposite end of the alley, in approximately the same spot where a mugger named Joe Chill had stood all those years ago.

Unlike Chill, this figure wore a suit—double-breasted, pin-striped, hand-tailored, and made of fabric as dark as the shadows around him. There was a snap-brim fedora perched on the top of his head. It was tilted forward, shrouding his face in darkness.

"Thought you might come here to mope about," he said, then chuckled.

Two other men waited in the shadows. It was a familiar tactic. I couldn't see them, but I could hear them breathing.

If I were anybody else, I'd be scared to death.

"Who are you?" I asked.

The man in the pin-striped suit and fedora ignored my question. "When you lose everything, I want you to remember the one who did this to you."

"A little hard to do if I don't know your name. You don't happen to have a business card, do you?"

"Right here," he said, lifting his head. "Bruce."

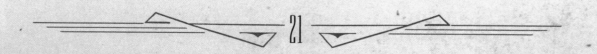

I WAS NOT BATMAN NOW.
I WAS MERELY BRUCE WAYNE.

The sodium lights from above revealed the man's face.

He had none.

The effect was startling. I hoped this sensation is what the predators of Gotham City feel when they see the Batman. Like my mask, the contours of his ebony visage were exaggerated and hid the real face beneath. But this mask was taken to a grotesque extreme. It looked like an obsidian statue of a fierce warrior who had melted while screaming, leaving this horrific fossil behind . . . dressed in a pin-striped suit and fedora.

"Who are you?" I asked.

"The Black Mask of Fate, Mr. Wayne. I've come for you at long last."

Then he nodded. I knew a signal would be coming. While the man in the suit was making his grand reveal, his minions silently flanked me like professional mercenaries. I could hear the rustle of their clothes. The soft sound of rubber soles on pavement. The Black Mask in front of me; his men to the left and right; and a graffiti-covered brick wall behind me. It was a classic trap.

His men charged.

This situation would not be a problem for the Batman. A simple leap and a roundhouse kick could take out both thugs easily. He could even be creative and use one thug's face as a human jackhammer on the other, leaving them to pick teeth out of the alley for an hour, wondering which molar belonged to which mouth.

But I was not Batman now. I was merely Bruce Wayne.

Bruce Wayne, billionaire playboy, might know a few cheap moves. Maybe a one-two Krav Maga combination, something you learn while messing around with a professional bodyguard in Aspen or Dubai—certainly nothing adequate for this assault.

So I let it come.

The thug on the right was all business. He hit me in the side of the head like he meant it. I anticipated the blow and went along with it, robbing it of some of its strength.

Unfortunately, I stumbled backward a few steps and collided with the thug at my left, who went for a few sloppy kidney shots. Fireworks went off inside my body. My heart rate leaped. I knew I would see blood in my urine later.

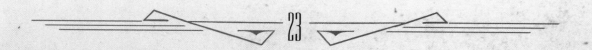

I fell to my knees and pretended to flail about wildly. But I knew exactly what shots I was landing on them. A couple of misses, one critical hit. I spaced them out enough to make it seem accidental, such as one solid punch to a thug's knees—on the side, the most vulnerable part. If the knee didn't fail entirely, he'd limp for the better part of the year.

He screamed.

His partner panicked and slammed a knee into the middle of my back. I fell forward on the thug with the brand-new bad knee.

The partner pulled me off, then grabbed me by the arms, twisting them behind my back until my wrists touched at an awkward angle. My arms still ached from the night before, which didn't help matters.

Black Mask shuffled toward me, enjoying the spectacle. Was it time for him to dirty his hands, now that his prey had been subdued?

"This has to be just right," he said, more to himself than to me.

Then his gloved fist smashed into my mouth.

"Yes, yes. Just like that."

Even I didn't see that coming. Usually a punch is telegraphed in your opponent's eyes. But it's hard to see what's coming when you're being hit by a man with no face.

My mouth felt like it had been stuffed with copper pennies. Now I was angry. By the time the next punch was on its way, I'd freed my left hand and I was able to stop Black Mask's fist, trapping it. He panicked and pulled back. I focused my grip on his index finger. He pulled frantically. I snapped the finger loose from its joint. He howled and retreated.

It was a lucky break for Bruce Wayne . . . until Black Mask swung back around, harder than before, and whipped his fist across my forehead.

The other thug let me go. I fell to the greasy alley floor and blinked the blood out of my eyes as the first kick landed in my rib cage. Then another. And another, flipping me around.

Then I felt fingers around my throat.

Black Mask stared down at me. I could feel his body heat radiating from under his mask and clothes. The sweat. The rage.

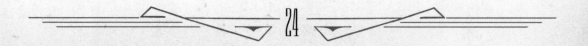

"All your buried secrets are about to come to light."

Then he left me to bleed.

I stared at the stars hanging above Gotham. The neon blur almost hid them from view. But they were still up there.

I listened to the Black Mask's footsteps as he made his way back down the alley along with his thugs. The click-click of expensive shoes; the dull thud of rubber soles.

The moment I was sure they were gone, I stood up and looked at the thing in my right hand: the first thug's wallet.

I had felt the bulge in the back of his pants when I landed on top of him. Never, ever carry your wallet to a job.

I opened it and found a Gotham City driver's license, set to expire next month. The name wasn't one I recognized; the face was unremarkable, although it was attached to an overly thick neck. There were a few singles. No personal photographs. Four credit cards—three of them for department stores, one for a hardware store. There was a card indicating that this sterling citizen was a member of the Gotham City Building and Trades Union.

Behind the singles, I found a folded piece of paper.

158 B

FOUND IN WALLET OF HENCHMAN

MAP OF MANOR AND GROUNDS

It was not a simple map that burglars would use to case a house; this map had geologic and topographical detail. Why would a hired thug need to know the elevation, land contours, and types of vegetation surrounding Wayne Manor?

This Black Mask and his men knew who I was. And they knew exactly where I lived, in vivid detail. They even knew where I mourned. Their arrival in the alley, mere hours after the discovery of the body, was no accident.

I needed answers.

And the man who could supply them was waiting for me at home.

# THE PARTY

"You ran off to get mugged before I had a chance to explain."

I tried not to wince, but I couldn't help it. Something about Alfred makes me feel like a little kid again.

Especially when he's running a polyglycolic suture through the tender flesh above my eye.

"I'm not going anywhere now," I said. "Ouch."

"Her name was Fiona Scott," Alfred said. "And until today, I thought she'd gone off to a new life somewhere. Somewhere to start over."

The name was vaguely familiar, but I couldn't place it.

That wasn't surprising. My father's life and times were my own personal Greek mythology. Names loomed larger than life; everything interesting seemed to have happened before I was born. After my parents were murdered, stories passed down to me through Alfred, and through my father's journal. I studied the people in them. I read about their adventures. I knew them all, like a child knows the names and stories of Hansel and Gretel, Cinderella, and Rumpelstiltskin.

But the adult context was missing, the way my father would have told me about his career

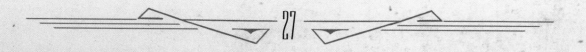

if he were alive today. There's a way you tell a ten-year-old about what you do, and the choices you've made. There's another way you tell a twenty-one-year-old the same stories.

"Miss Fiona Scott," Alfred continued, "was your father's first secretary at Wayne Enterprises."

That was it. I remembered now. She was a minor player, but still a member of the pantheon.

"Are you sure it's the same woman?"

"I am, Master Bruce. The necklace was one of the first things you noticed about her attire—she never took it off, even when it failed to match her dress or shoes."

"And you notice these things all the time."

"I am English, sir."

"What was she like?"

"Beautiful."

I stared at Alfred.

"Just stating a fact. Everyone at the company had a bit of a crush on Miss Scott. But the irony was that Miss Scott only had eyes for her employer."

"My father."

"Dr. Wayne would joke about it. He'd tell her, 'You know I am married, Miss Scott. And with a newborn son, no less. What could you possibly see in a boring old war vet like me?'"

I released some air I suddenly realized I'd been gathering in my lungs.

"Master Bruce?"

"I thought you were headed somewhere else, Alfred."

"Your mother had nothing to worry about. There are few truly faithful men in this world. I've had the pleasure of serving one of them." Alfred allowed his gaze to linger.

"Critique noted," I said. "Tell me more about her. Namely, who would want to hurt her."

"No one," Alfred said. "But many wanted to possess her."

I thought about the card the police found on the body. "There was one in particular, wasn't there?"

"There is a name that immediately springs to mind, yes." Alfred finished stitching my eyebrow, then settled in to tell me about Cameron Brady.

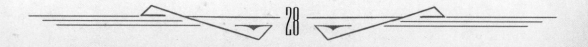

His name was another familiar one. Cameron Brady was a young executive at Wayne Enterprises—one of my father's first hires, Alfred reminded me. Brady considered my father a mentor of sorts, and he used to hang around his office a lot, just to talk. That must have been where he first met Fiona Scott. And then he started hanging around the office just to talk to Fiona.

"Miss Scott was flattered, your father told me. At first. But Mr. Brady's affections were never returned. At least not in the way he'd imagined. I remember your father wrestling over having to say something to Mr. Brady—his attention to Miss Scott was bordering on harassment. Dr. Wayne never liked to meddle in the personal lives of his employees, but eventually he came to see it as a pressing business matter."

Alfred explained that everything came to a head about a year later at the Wayne family's annual ball. Then he handed me an invitation, which included a short list of featured honorees. They were other surnames from the Wayne pantheon: Ardai. Banks. Hughes. Pavia. Resnick. Sionis. Wellington. My father's peers. Gotham's elite.

Right up until my parents were murdered, I attended those parties. I was always sent to the children's room, where there were candied apples and popcorn and entertainers—usually clowns. God, how I hated those clowns. I would always wonder what was going on in the main hall.

"Mr. Brady was there, in costume," Alfred said. "But even though he was masked I could tell that he was quite intoxicated."

"Wait," I said. "It was a costume party?"

Alfred paused for a moment. "How odd, I never realized it before. Of course you were only two years old, off to bed early and too young to remember."

"What do you mean?"

Alfred handed me a photo snapped at the party. It showed two couples wearing masks. Scrawled in blue ink at the bottom were their names: Thomas, Martha, Fredric, Dorothy. The first two were my parents. The others were the Sionises, who used to own a high-end cosmetics company based in Gotham. The Janus Corporation. *Très* glamorous.

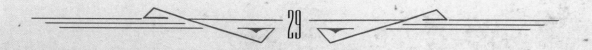

I stared at the photograph.

This was not a familiar image from the Wayne mythology that I knew.

I have often wondered what my father—a decorated war doctor and self-made billionaire—would think of his only son dressing up in a bat costume, hiding behind reinforced fabrics, capes, gloves, and boots. Would he look at my visage—which was meant to terrify—and merely laugh? Or would he shake his head sadly, unable to understand where he'd gone wrong?

But here was my father, wearing a black bat mask, obscuring his face except for the area around his mouth and his eyes. Those eyes looked up from the faded photograph, right into my soul.

Did I see my father that night? Did he lift me up into his arms, give me a hug goodnight, all the while wearing that mask?

Did I dream about that mask?

*Am I still dreaming about that mask?*

Until that moment, I thought my obsession with the form of the bat had developed years later. Here it was though, in its infancy. My infancy.

But I couldn't think about that now.

I looked at Alfred. "What happened at the party? Was Fiona Scott there?"

"Indeed."

Fiona Scott became ill a few months before the party, and she had been away at a clinic upstate, Alfred explained. ("Your father paid for her care in its entirety.") But since returning to work, Fiona had been withdrawn. She was pale, fragile, and depressed. She snapped at people, which was completely unlike her. "Your father had to practically beg her to attend the party—which she did reluctantly, I must say."

Later, as the party wound down, Alfred explained that he saw my father escorting Fiona to a patio behind Wayne Manor. They seemed to be having an intense conversation.

"I do not know what was discussed," Alfred said. "I never asked. And that was the last time I saw Miss Scott. Later, your father told me she'd gone back to live with her mother in Houston."

"Whatever it was," I said, "could it have involved Brady?"

"That possibility has been on my mind, I'm afraid."

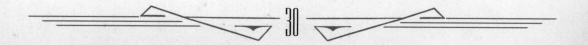

RECEIVED FROM ALFRED PENNYWORTH

(LEFT TO RIGHT) MARTHA WAYNE,

THOMAS WAYNE, FREDRIC SIONIS,

I WOULD ALWAYS WONDER WHAT WAS
GOING ON IN THE MAIN HALL.

"Were they together at the party?"

"Not that I could tell. Mr. Brady was, shall we say, enjoying the spirits of the evening a bit too much."

"I need to talk to him."

"No," Alfred said.

"No?"

"I took the liberty of making a few inquiries. Cameron Brady retired from Wayne Enterprises a decade ago and died from a premature heart attack a few years later."

I considered this. "Wait—what about my father's journals? Call the university."

I keep my father's journals at the research wing of the Gotham University Library. A burglar can take anything he wants from Wayne Manor—though God help his soul if I catch him in the act. But my father's journals are too great a loss to even ponder.

They were the only link I had to his voice, which grew fainter with each passing year.

"After you left so—ahem— abruptly, I took the liberty of retrieving the volume with the dates that correspond to the party."

"Good work, Alfred."

"However, the entry from that night is missing."

"What?"

"The pages seem to have been ripped completely out of the book, as you'll see. I've placed the rest of the volume downstairs in your . . . study."

I thought about the party, and Fiona Scott, and Cameron Brady. I thought about my father in that bat mask.

What did he see that night, through those eyeholes?

"Something bothers me about this," I said.

"I should think so."

"No. Not that. It's what my friend in the black mask said tonight. 'All of your buried secrets are about to come to light.' As if he knew what the workmen would find. Which means that he is someone old enough to remember that party."

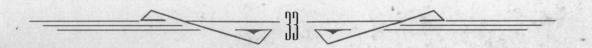

"It is curious," Alfred admitted.

"But who could it have been?"

"What a fortunate thing it is that you are a professional detective, Master Bruce." Alfred stood up. "I will fetch your father's journal for you."

## THE WAYNES

I rarely visit my parents' graves.

If I'm in a mood to sink down into the darkness and pain, to rip open the mental scars, I visit Crime Alley.

Now, though, I had a good reason to visit.

*All your buried secrets are about to come to light.*

The Wayne family mausoleum is half a mile away from home. Alfred visits fairly regularly, tending to the grounds—even though they have people for that. He leaves a bottle of my father's favorite scotch on the marble step leading up to the vault on his birthday. Alfred tells me that the cemetery staff has caught on in the past few years. Instead of resting for a few weeks, the bottle now disappears almost immediately. I don't think my father would have minded; he always loved giving gifts.

He would mind, however, that the Wayne family burial place had been recently desecrated.

I stood there in the humid grass of the cemetery and stared at the bronze doors of the vault, which was a formidable mass of marble and bronze. There were dents and scratches and hash marks along the edge of one of the doors.

Why would a man break into my parents' vault?

Why would he bury the body of a young woman in the front lawn of Wayne Manor?

Why would he do that to them?

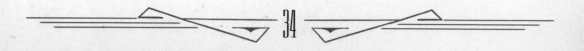

WHY WOULD A MAN BREAK
INTO MY PARENTS' VAULT?

I felt the rage coming up from that secret place inside me. This was yet another violation. People should be able to live their lives without being senselessly gunned down in a dirty alley. And if they die prematurely, their resting places should be sacrosanct—undisturbed, for all ages. The peace that was stolen from my parents in life was now torn from them again in death.

I wanted whoever did this to pay.

But no. It was not the time.

I inhaled, exhaled. I focused on breathing. Finding the balance. My years in Tibet taught me that much.

I remembered what Alfred said: *You are a professional detective.*

So I started acting like one.

I walked up to the doors, examining them carefully. I could see the tiny pieces of shaved metal. Somebody had worked the doors with a crowbar. Hard.

There were muddy footprints leading into the vault, and then away. Whoever had broken in had not bothered to clean up or disguise the break-in. I took note of the prints' size and shape.

I stepped inside. I had never before been inside the vault. I was now so close to my parents after twenty years of . . . nothing.

I took a moment to focus, to breathe.

The air was musty. It felt like I was swallowing giant gulps of the past with every breath.

Two spaces on the left hold the bodies of my parents. There's a space on the right meant for me. When my war is over, this is where they'll put my body. Maybe by that time I'll deserve that space alongside my parents.

But the slab of stone, sealing my future resting place, had been broken in half.

*What happened here, Dad? Did you see who did it? Did you ask them why?*

I needed air. I needed to breathe. To think.

I sat down on the front steps of the mausoleum and pulled out my father's journal. I needed to hear his voice in my head, reassuring me.

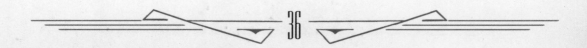

158 B

PAGE FROM THOMAS WAYNE'S JOURNAL

SHAME AND GUILT?

I tried to remember that moment. Impossible, I know, considering I was only two. But it was amazing to imagine a time in my life when I was innocent and free and could run into my father's office at home and smile at him and he'd stop what he was doing, just to spend time with me. Even though something was weighing on his mind.

Fiona Scott.

My eyes focused on the words "shame and guilt." What did he mean by that? What did Fiona have to be ashamed of?

Something out in the graveyard flashed with a popping sound.

I looked up, scanning the field of pale headstones in the dark. Something flashed again. Harsh. Painful.

Whoever it was started running. So I followed.

Here I was again, doing the job of Batman while dressed as Bruce Wayne. I knew I should hold myself back, but I couldn't. I needed to find out who was behind this nightmare. The running man might give me answers.

I leapt over headstones. I twisted my body around oversized crosses. I could hear my prey breathing hard. Panting. Grunting with exertion.

He made it ten yards before I tackled him into the dirt. A black box went spinning out of his hands. I heard glass shatter.

"Don't hurt me!"

I flipped him over by his clothes. The little bit of moonlight in the sky revealed some of his features. At least it wasn't another man in a mask. His lips trembled.

"Who are you?"

"M-Mike Zimmerman. With the *Gotham Globe.*"

A newspaper reporter?

I looked at the black box that had spun out of his hands. It was the body of a camera, its flashbulb shattered.

Correction.

He was a newspaper photographer.

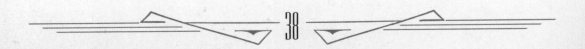

I moved back, allowing him to sit up. Zimmerman made a show of coughing and touched his neck, as if he'd be able to feel a fracture. This was going to be tricky. Too many celebrities had punched, kicked, and tackled too many paparazzi over the years. "Why are you here?" I asked.

"You know, you're a lot faster than you look. You scared the hell out of me. I thought you rich guys were—"

"Tell me what you're doing at my parents' gravesite."

"I could ask you the same question, Wayne. Been a big night for you, hasn't it? I figured I'd catch you here."

"Nobody knew I was coming here."

"Well, yeah. But I have a right to protect my sources." He got up on his hands and knees and patted the ground. "You own any camera shops, Wayne? Because it'll probably be cheaper than the bill I'll send you for repairing and cleaning this baby. It's a Pentax. My good one, too."

I walked away from Zimmerman, tuning him out. Continuing the conversation was pointless; he'd been tipped off.

What's worse is that I fell right into Black Mask's trap. His corny line about buried secrets had done the trick. I'd gone straight to the graveyard, right where he wanted me.

I was in the junior league, all over again.

A quick anonymous call to the *Globe* pays off either way: Zimmerman either finds billionaire Bruce Wayne breaking into his parents' vault or finds the evidence of a break-in thereafter.

Again, the questions nagged me.

Why?

Who stands to benefit?

And *when will they stop*?

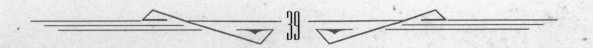

# THE FRIEND

"Let me guess." Roman Sionis flipped to the *Gotham Globe*'s front cover. The headline was in large bold type:

*BODY OF YOUNG WOMAN UNEARTHED AT WAYNE MANOR*

"Is that what happened to your eye?" Roman asked, pointing to my stitches and smiling. "One of your girlfriends got too wild? Here I thought you were busy punching out members of the fourth estate."

Roman pointed to a smaller headline lower down.

*REACTION! RED-EYED BILLIONAIRE ASSAULTS GLOBE PHOTOG*

Even after all these years, I still want to punch Roman in the face whenever he smiles.

It was the day after the discovery in the front lawn. Roman and I were at a cocktail table on the deck of the *Aubrey James*, permanently moored in Gotham Harbor. A 100-year-old, four-masted steel barque, once used to haul coal and nitrate from Wales to South America, it had been retrofitted into a playground for Gotham's elite and renamed after the man who was mayor when my parents were killed. It was the club my father referred to in his journal. I hadn't been here in months.

This spot was one of Roman's favorites, because his father, Fredric, used to own it. Roman still acted like the ship was part of the Sionis fleet, even though Roman's family bankruptcy had released it a few years prior.

"What can I say, Roman? I lead an active life. But so do you." I flipped the newspaper back around to him and tapped a small story near the bottom:

*ALLEGED "HEIR" DROPS CLAIM TO JANUS FORTUNE*

"What happened?" I asked. "Another brother of yours pop up?"

Roman used a modeling kit's soldering iron to melt its face and burn holes in the parachute. "Napalm attack!" he screamed. I had no idea what that meant until years later.

When my parents died, the Sionises attended the funeral. Roman stuck out his tongue at me. Not in jest, or to make me laugh, but in imitation of someone who'd been strangled. Or murdered.

We all grew up.

Years later, the Janus Corporation hit the skids; Fredric Sionis killed himself in his office at home. After his wife discovered the body, she swallowed a bottle and a half of pills. A burning cigarette that fell out of her hand took care of the mansion, setting it ablaze. A hundred years of Gotham history—gone in a few hours. Roman, only twenty-six-years old, inherited the company and presided over its downward spiral.

Wayne Enterprises eventually bailed it out with a series of loans, which spared the company from certain death. It hummed along now—and Gotham was better off maintaining its industries.

But Roman never forgave me for it.

"What are you drinking?" he asked, smirking.

"If you're buying, something at least sixteen years old and single-malt," I said.

"Nice. Still trying to impress the ladies, are we?"

"Nah. If I wanted to do that, I'd fire up something Cuban."

"Many young ladies have told me that kissing a smoker is like licking a charcoal briquette."

I smiled. "Well, I must have found the ones who really love their barbecue."

This talk about women was typical with Roman. It was compensation. He was a handsome enough guy—but somehow, his personality always came oozing through the cracks to ruin everything. You could see the spite on his face, even when he was trying to smile.

Roman smiled now. He had his right hand tucked into the breast of his suit—always something light-colored, no matter the season.

"So what's shaking, Brucie? Need a little brotherly advice?"

"I'd like to jog your memory a bit," I said. "Do you remember a party at my parents' house years ago? When we were kids, I mean."

"My parents always dragged me to your parents' boring parties. No offense."

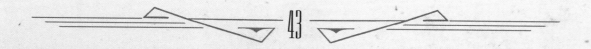

"None taken."

"Which one would this be?"

"A costume party, back when you were about eight."

I showed him the photo of our parents. Thomas. Martha. Fredric. Dorothy. Smiling, masked. Roman's face tightened as he looked at it.

I couldn't tell which couple set him off: my parents or his. As I got older, I'd come to realize that the Sionises secretly hated my parents and would bad-mouth them any chance they got—even after my parent's deaths, when they were unable to defend themselves. That explained many of the strange looks I received in certain circles whenever I'd say my last name. I don't know precisely what was said; I could only guess that the rumors involved multiple infidelities on my father's part and the bitter jealousy of my mother. My lifestyle didn't help matters, of course. Every time the *Globe* reported on another fling (half of them fabricated, the other half exaggerated), I could almost hear the whispers: Like father, like son.

"I think I do remember this one," Roman said, turning the photograph upside down, then sliding it back across the table to me. "There I was, thinking I was going to a Halloween party. But instead, I was stuck in a stuffy old mansion in the little kids' room while the adults next door guzzled martinis and made sloppy passes at each other. No wonder we all drink so much these days. Look at our role models!"

"Did your dad ever say anything to you about this party?"

"No," Roman said. "Did yours?"

"I was too young."

"Weren't we all."

I looked out over Miller Harbor, with Finger River beyond. The evening wind rippled over the water, sun dancing on the waves. The city could seem peaceful, if you knew where to look.

"Say, Bruce—what's this about anyway? Did old man Pennyworth find a martini stain in the study and start looking for someone to blame after all these years?"

I tapped the *Gotham Globe* and frowned. "No, it's this. Alfred recognized the woman. She used to work for my father and was last seen alive at that party I mentioned."

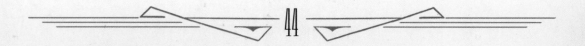

"Oh."

"Do you remember her?"

"What did you say her name was?"

"I didn't," I said, watching his eyes carefully. "Fiona Scott."

Roman rolled his eyes in the appropriate direction—the left, which indicates truthful recollection, rather than crafty fabrication. "Nah, can't say I do." Then he leaned in conspiratorially and smirked. "Was she hot?"

For the second time in ten minutes, I wanted to punch him in the face.

"You need to lighten up, Brucie baby. Seriously."

"Your father keep any journals, by chance?" I asked.

"My dad? Uh, no. He was too busy running our family business into the ground. But you know what? I think I know the next best thing. My father's manservant—Abbott. He's down in Old Gotham, in some elder-care facility, but trust me, the man's still sharp as a pigsticker. Remembers every damn thing. If somebody knows anything about that party, it's him."

"I'd very much like to speak to him."

"I'll have my secretary send you his contact info."

"Can't you write it out for me?" I asked. "Or are you too busy at the moment?"

Roman grunted. He disguised it as a cough, but it was the same kind of grunt he'd given when I used to tell him to leave my toy soldiers alone, right before he'd snap off one of their heads.

"Oh—and make sure you print," I added. "If I recall, your handwriting's atrocious."

He took a coaster from the table and scribbled a few notes on the back.

"The ladies don't complain when I give them my number."

"Oh? They're old enough to read?"

Another smile. Acidic enough to corrode a steal beam. Roman slid the coaster to me.

"Thanks for your help," I said.

"Anything for a friend."

I looked down at the notes and quickly studied them.

Of course.

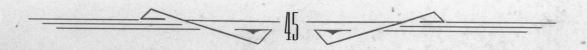

158 B

AUBREY JAMES COASTER

ROMAN'S HANDWRITING

# THE KILLERS

"Elder-care facility" was a euphemism. It was the waiting room in Hell, and its occupants were the damned and forsaken.

I found Ethan Abbott in a rust-pocked wheelchair in the hallway. The walls were industrial white, which is to say, a vertigo-inducing shade of gray. The stench of bodily fluids was enough to gag me. This was the place where bodies broke down and died. The only benefit of aging such a place was that your senses were dulled enough not to notice it . . . much.

"Mr. Abbott?"

His eyes were pale, his skin raw. He looked like he'd been exposed to toxic fumes for a few minutes, every morning, for months on end.

"Yes, SIR."

I told the old man who I was, and who'd sent me. Why I was here.

"Oh yes. I remember everything. In perfect detail. You'll see."

"You do?"

Abbott blinked as if he'd been slapped.

"Of COURSE I do! Just because you find me here in this pit of despair does not mean my faculties have entirely departed, sir!"

"I didn't mean to imply . . ."

"Your mother . . . oh, your mother. I would have liked to have had the chance to club her to death for what she did to that poor woman."

I looked at the doorway next to him. The name plate was empty. Inside, the bed was stripped down to its thin, stained mattress. There were two cardboard boxes, advertising popular brands of potato chips on the side, full of odds and ends. The closet door was open. Empty, except for a few cheap wire hangers.

"My mother," I said.

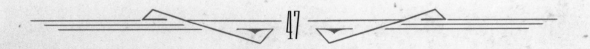

THIS WAS THE PLACE WHERE
BODIES BROKE DOWN AND DIED.

"YOUR MOTHER!" he bellowed. "Sir."

"Tell me what she did."

"Oh, such bitterness. And rage. Plenty of rage! The jealousy. I'm telling you I've never seen such a horrifying visage as I did that night. I saw it all."

"You did no such thing," I said.

"I DID! I was standing in the pantry, you see, opening another case of Champagne. Your father had taken audience with that young girl out on the patio, just a few yards away. She was wailing and caterwauling about something, and your father was yelling at her, telling her no, things didn't work that way in his world. Which is to say our world. The REAL WORLD!"

"Go on."

"And then . . . out of the corner of my eye, I saw the wench. Your mother. She spied the two of them. Your father's big hands on the girl's little spindly arms. Shaking them. It must have driven your mother completely mad. She picked up the closest weapon—a wrought iron flower stand, I think—and crept up behind the girl. And then she screamed. She screamed your father's name, and then she struck her directly in the head."

"My mother," I said.

"YOUR MOTHER!" he bellowed again. "Are you deaf as well as stupid? Oh, you should have seen them. The rich at play. When the rage had cooled, they remembered their social standing, and how this could bring their world down around them. So they wrapped the body in a tarp and brought it out to the family mausoleum, where no one would ever think to look for it. Your mother faked a letter. Everyone believed it. EVERYONE!"

"Mr. Abbott," I said, "then why did workmen find the body on the grounds of Wayne Manor?"

"Oh, you canny one! You should know that . . . because you REBURIED HER THERE! Thought you'd get rid of her forever! Making room for your own self in that creepy family VAULT of yours!"

Other residents of the rest home were now looking in our direction.

"Yes, I know all about it, Bruce Wayne, and don't think I'm not going to call the police. Your days as a free man are OVER!"

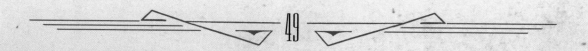

I put a hand on his thin, bony shoulder and looked him in the eyes.

"Thank you, Mr. Abbott," I said. "That was perfect."

"You're welcome."

As I turned to leave, he grabbed my sleeve.

"So, how soon, then? Did Roman say?"

"Soon," I told him. "Very, very soon."

# THE SECOND SON

Evening fell over Gotham. I pondered the clues I'd gathered. Listened to the voices in my head.

My visit with Roman had given me an unexpected lead. The follow-up with his father's butler had cleared up a great deal. It was all starting to fit together.

Except for the *why*.

People claim to read and enjoy mysteries for the whodunnit factor—figuring out the identity of the killer behind the mask. But to me, infinitely more interesting is the *why*: the chain of events, the personal apocalypses, the miniature tragedies that lie at the root of all crimes.

I knew the identity of my nemesis. I did not know why, after all these years, he'd chosen to come after me.

It was time to pay Gordon a visit and hear what he'd discovered over the past twenty-four hours. Then I'd share my findings—or most of them—with him. That's how our relationship works. Give and take. He views me as a mysterious benefactor; someone war-weary who's seen more than his share of bloodshed and, for some reason, has chosen Gotham as his home. If only he knew the truth.

I was suiting up when Alfred entered the Batcave.

"Surely there's an easier way to deliver a message to the authorities," he said.

"Gordon likes it when I dress formally."

And then I was off, in my mask and cape and suit, speeding through the dark streets of

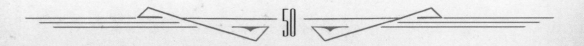

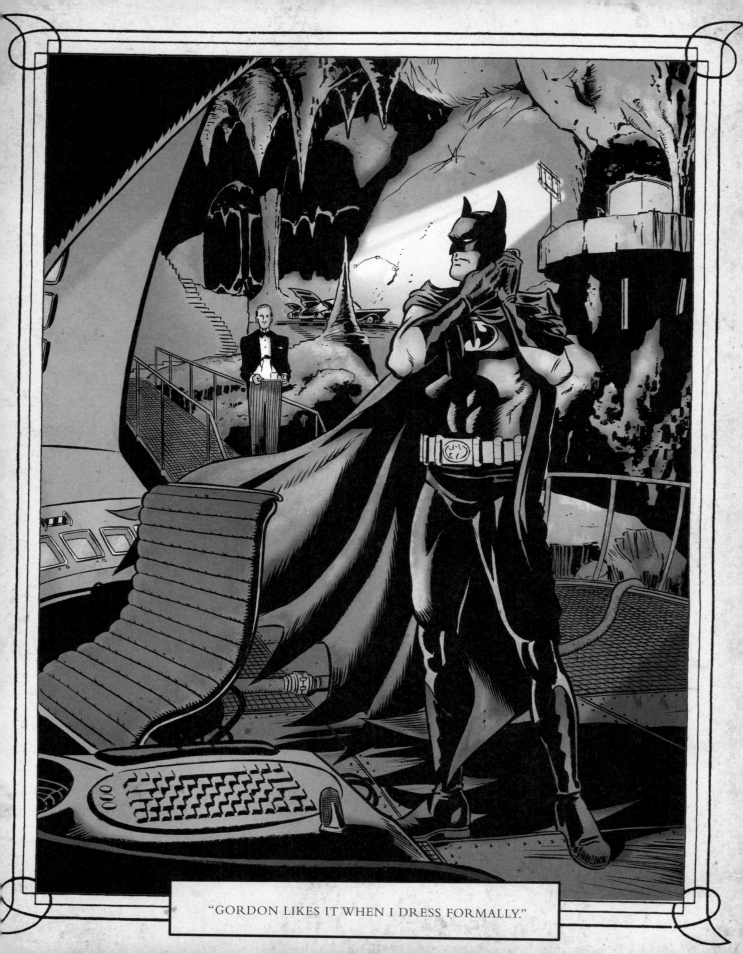

"GORDON LIKES IT WHEN I DRESS FORMALLY."

Gotham, neon melting, stars hidden, my pulse racing . . . trying hard to avoid the bitter memory traps along the way . . .

To Jim Gordon, I simply materialized in the backseat of his Gotham City PD issued unmarked sedan like a phantom.

"Mother of—"

What he didn't see was the speedy detective work, the surveillance, the lock-picking, and the utter silence required to achieve the effect.

"One of these days, it isn't going to be you," Gordon said.

"Her name was Fiona Scott," I said.

Gordon's jaw dropped. "How did you . . . "

I said nothing. Better to preserve the mystery.

Gordon shook his head. "Well, we came up with the same name. Dental records, cross-checked with Wayne Enterprises employee files. Figured we'd start at the company, then take it wide." He coughed. "We also received an anonymous phone call a couple of hours ago, giving us the name."

I grunted. "There's a lot of that going around."

"Indeed there is. So what do you know about Ms. Scott?"

"She was last seen at a swank party at Wayne Manor twenty-eight years ago."

"That we didn't know," Gordon said. "We had her disappearing in Houston."

"Texas?"

"Uh-huh. Relatives say she came home from her big job in Gotham City a disappointed, depressed girl. She split one night, left her mom a note, told her not to worry."

"Interesting."

"Not as interesting as this." Gordon held out an envelope. "An, um, anonymous donor dropped it off."

I took the envelope. It was stained yellow in the corners and made of a kind of paper too expensive to be widely used these days. It had to be at least thirty years old.

The return address was a health clinic upstate. Inside was a letter from one doctor to another—Dr. Thomas Wayne.

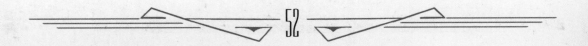

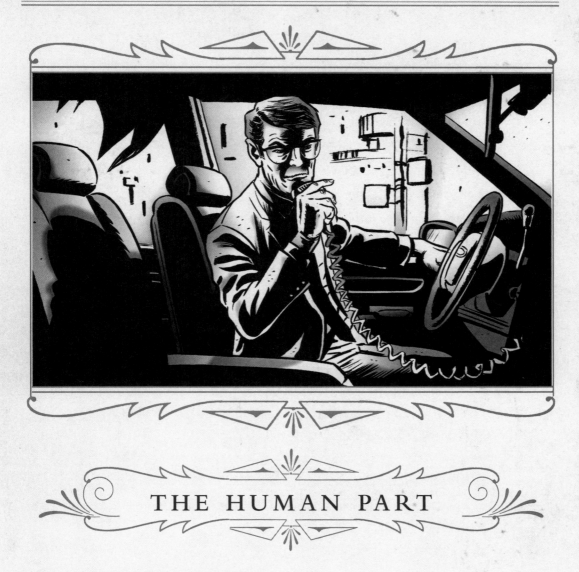

# THE HUMAN PART

I raced back to Wayne Manor.

Usually I take great pains to avoid appearing in the suit anywhere near home—disguises are about context as much as they are fabric and makeup and masks. One doesn't expect to see the partial face of Bruce Wayne, billionaire playboy, swinging down from a rooftop in the ghettoes of Gotham. One might be able to place it here, though, across the water, in the peaceful suburbs.

But there was no time for caution. Things were spiraling out of control. This wasn't about a crime in the distant past. This was about someone killing innocent people now.

Someone who wore a grotesque black mask.

And it grieved me to think about the man behind that mask.

There's something my own mask has: a built-in police scanner. I heard the updates on the way. The body was identified—a man named Matthew Foster. Blunt force trauma to the face.

Matt Foster. The foreman of the construction crew working on the grounds at Wayne Manor.

Black Mask's end game was slowly surfacing. I knew what he was doing.

*This has to be just right*, he had said as his goon held me up and he whipped his fist across my face.

If I were to park in the Batcave, change out of my suit, then pop out of the front doors of Wayne Manor . . . what would the Gotham Police see? A billionaire with fresh stitches over his eye and purple and tan bruises on his face . . . in close proximity to a man who had been killed by blunt force trauma. The same man who was responsible for discovering a corpse that could bring shame to the billionaire's family.

And somewhere, nearby, would be a murder weapon. Perhaps a shovel. Or a candleholder. A bronze fireplace poker.

Or a wrought iron flower holder.

The motive, the means, the murder weapon.

This had all been planned in great detail. All I needed to do was show up.

The Batmobile roared down the road approaching the manor. Funny, I'd never driven the vehicle around the front. Everything was out of context.

Then the right rear tire exploded.

The vehicle is designed for such things. It was originally built for the military by Wayne Enterprises, able to traverse any terrain—even roads blown to chunks—on as few as two tires.

I hammered the brakes and skidded the Batmobile to a sideways stop. Not because I had to. But because I wanted to meet the man who'd fired the shot.

He'd be nearby. No doubt about it. Watching the scene. Planning for contingencies.

But did he expect something like me?

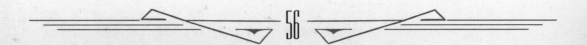

The top of the Batmobile popped open with a pneumatic hiss. I jumped out and landed, spreading my full cape around me. Like animals that puff up, it gives my opponents a false sense of my size. I want them to feel intimidated.

"You," a voice hissed. "What are you doing here?"

A figure stepped out of the shadows. It was, of course, Black Mask—the same man I'd encountered the night before.

"I was out for a drive."

"Thought you only prowled the mean streets, freak," he said. "Not the suburbs."

"Nice suit," I said.

"This old thing? Just something I had lying around. Not as interesting as what you're wearing."

"You always dress up to assault innocent people?"

"Innocent!" Black Mask cried. "Who's innocent? The billionaire beyond this fence? Hardly. His is the biggest crime of all. Bruce Wayne has blood on his hands. Go see for yourself."

"No. You're the killer."

"You're wrong. You and I are exactly alike. I've read a lot about you. You never kill, even when your victims desperately deserve it. Me neither. I just do my part for justice."

"Maybe it's time I change my policy."

It was the same scene playing out again—distract your prey while your hunters surround him. I heard rustling in the bushes. Footfalls on the earth. There were more of them now. Black Mask had expanded his team. I could sense at least half a dozen.

More of a fight this time.

Beneath my cape, my right hand fell to one of my two Batropes. And in my left hand: two concussion grenades—enough smoke and fury to throw even a military sniper off target.

Just a little something to take care of the hired help.

"I told you I don't kill," Black Mask said.

Then, movement.

This is where he surprised me. The assault didn't come from the sides. It came from dead ahead. From Black Mask himself.

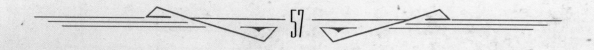

IT ALMOST FELT AS IF THE BULLETS WERE
RIPPING THROUGH MY OWN SKIN.

I dropped the rope and grenades and grabbed my cape.

This is when it's most useful.

It's not very good for gliding, unless I plan ahead. It's moderately successful when it comes to intimidating criminals. But when it comes to obscuring my body while some nutcase is shooting bullets at me, there's nothing better.

I anticipated the shots as best I could and banked in the opposite direction. I heard the spinning projectiles rip through the fabric. It almost felt as if the bullets were ripping through my own skin.

I dropped to the ground, as flat as I could be without lying down, and snatched up one of the grenades. I rose, ramrod as a cornfield scarecrow, and whipped the grenade toward Black Mask.

Directly at his grotesque face.

BOOM!

He howled, hands to his head, trying to make the hurt go away.

At that precise moment his hired help came screaming out of the shadows, intending to rip me to pieces.

This wasn't about one man versus half a dozen trained fighters. This was about me having multiple targets for a variety of assaults.

This was me—in my element.

A punch to someone's throat. An elbow lock; a fist to a chin. The Batrope around three pairs of legs; a roundhouse kick at three skulls. Piston-fast punches. The sensation of ribs cracking beneath my fist. Again. And again. And again. And again.

A psychiatrist might wonder if I imagine Joe Chill, my parents' murderer, whenever I deliver punishment to those who deserve it. I don't. I see a monster, the ultimate city predator—the nightmare silhouette that is familiar to anyone who's ever been mugged. Ever been attacked. Ever watched their loved ones suffer and die. Once I have that image in my mind, the rest is easy. My job is to take apart the monster, one bone-snapping punch at a time.

What holds me back from absolute fury is that once I kill—once I push, hit, slap, gouge, snap, break, pummel a bit too far—then it is over. I become Chill. Then I become the monster.

So I hold back, and I let it all go at the same time.

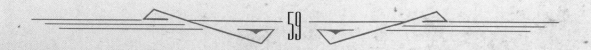

This tenuous balance has taken me years to achieve. And it will probably take me the rest of my life to perfect.

When it was over, I found Black Mask trying to crawl away. He was moaning. I used my boot to flip him onto his back.

His mask now sported a huge crack in the middle. Whatever it was made of could break under pressure. The shock of the grenade had hit him hard. The mask's nose was completely gone. I could see human skin beneath the fissures and cracks. I could also see a tiny stream of blood flowing down his neck.

"I would have hoped you'd punish the real killer," he said, his voice trembling. "Bruce Wayne. Like father, like son. Do you realize what sins have been committed in that house?"

The man behind the mask had stopped his acting. It was his real voice now. Easy for me to recognize.

"It's clear that you don't have the heart," he said.

Too late I saw the pistol, still in his hand.

BLAM!

The blast hit me directly in the middle of the chest and flung me backward. I skidded on the grass.

"You should have stayed out of my business, Batman."

Black Mask climbed to this feet and staggered over, gun in hand. He looked down at me and saw that I was still alive. He grunted, lifted the pistol, and aimed it at my mouth.

The human part of my mask.

There's a design and purpose for everything in the Batsuit. The cape, the mask, the utility belt. Even the insignia on my chest—which is actually reinforced Level VIII body armor, double the strength of what the most heavily protected soldiers wear. The insignia isn't because I'm vain. The insignia is a target.

If you're going to shoot me anywhere, aim for the big yellow and black bat.

My mouth is another story.

Which is why I whipped my Batrope around Black Mask's gun hand, then yanked it to the

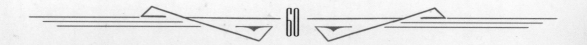

side. He fired. The bullet cut into the grass and dirt a few inches to the left of my shoulder.

Then I pulled down. Hard.

My gloved right fist was ready.

It found my opponent, shattering his mask completely.

He howled again. Whatever punishment my grenade had delivered, this pain was worse. We reversed positions, with me now on top. I picked away the shards of mask and stared into the face of my opponent.

*Roman Sionis.*

I had known, even yesterday, on the deck of the *Aubrey James*—as we were flashing our teeth at each other and listening to jazz and ordering single-malt scotches—that Roman was the man behind the mask.

But the questioned remained. . . . Why?

I can understand why he loathed Bruce Wayne. I was a convenient distraction from his personal troubles. I was younger. Richer. Dated more attractive women (at least according to what's reported in the *Globe*). Better to hold me up as evidence that life is unfair than confront his own weaknesses.

Was that enough for him to don a grotesque mask and an absurd gangster suit and assault me in an alley? And frame my parents for murder?

I had a theory. It was time to find out if it was correct.

"This isn't your business!" Roman hissed at me, still unaware it was his old childhood buddy Bruce beneath the mask. Roman's eyes, bloodshot, tearing and wild, focused on the inhuman part. The ears. The molded forehead. Not the man beneath.

"I've just made it my business."

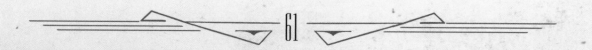

I punched him in the face again. It felt good.

There was no time for any fancy materializations. No appearing in a cloud of mist. Jim Gordon saw me coming all the way. Saw me dragging Roman Sionis across the front lawn of Wayne Manor.

The police on the scene were quick. Weapons were drawn, pointed at my center of gravity: the ruined bat symbol on my chest.

"Good Lord," Gordon said, motioning for his officers to stand down. "What did you do to that man?"

"Trust me," I said. "He's looked worse."

"Who is he?"

I told him.

Gordon didn't believe me. "Isn't one bad guy billionaire enough for one evening?"

"Any sign of Wayne?"

"No. And that's the funny part. Yesterday he joked about not fleeing the country, but now nobody seems to know where he is—not even his butler up there. You know what I think? I think he fled the country."

"Wayne is innocent," I said. "Someone is trying to frame him and his father."

Gordon exhaled. I could understand his hesitation. Here he was, on the front lawn of a super-rich murder suspect who seemed to have beaten a man to death because he uncovered evidence that the super-rich man's father bludgeoned a young woman to death after bearing his illegitimate child. "I don't suppose you have proof?" he asked.

"I will. If you give me one thing."

"What's that?"

"A blood sample from the murder victim."

Gordon guffawed. I don't think I ever really heard a guffaw until that moment.

"I wouldn't ask unless it was important."

After a few moments, Gordon nodded. What else could he do, really?

I asked him to book Sionis and wait to hear from me.

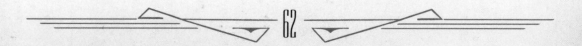

There. There it was.

I was not surprised at the results.

Saddened, maybe. But not surprised.

There was one more task to complete.

The Janus Corporation is a financially troubled company, despite the help Wayne Enterprises has given it over the years. Security at its headquarters in downtown Gotham, though, still appeared to be very well funded. Roman's a paranoid guy. Then again I'd take precautions, too, if I went around dressing up in a Halloween mask trying to ruin people's lives.

There was a mini-battalion of six uniformed, armed guards on the lobby level. At least a dozen more were roving the building, looking for intruders. Three more sat in the security office, eyes trained on monitors. Understandable. Roman could write off everything in the name of protecting his company's "trade secrets," as if it were likely that the invading hordes of a rival cosmetics company would wage bloody war on their competitor, one floor at a time.

These guards didn't worry me. I would be entering another way.

I rappelled down the smooth, vertical wall of the concrete facing, then positioned myself in front of my target window and placed one foot on either side of it. I bent both knees and pushed back as hard as possible. For a moment, I was flying through the air, attached to the building by a thin, strong cord.

The next . . .

My boots sailed cleanly through the glass. The windows imploded inward—no risk to passersby thirty floors below. A headache for the Janus Corporation's cleaning staff, but with Roman at the top, some smashed glass was the least of their worries.

I scanned Roman's office. Now, where would he hide it?

Thirty seconds later I found the vault in the first place I should have looked. It was behind a painted portrait of Roman's father—the founder of the Janus Corporation. *Hello, Fredric. Hope you are enjoying your eternal rest while the rest of us tidy up. If you see the Devil, give him my regards.*

The painting cast aside, I studied at the steel vault, hidden within a cutout of the wall. I paused, deciding what to pull out of my utility belt.

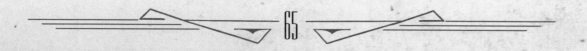

That's when three of the roving guards burst in, guns drawn.

"Hey!"

Roman apparently passed out firearms to every employee of the Janus Corporation. I'd hate to see what his executive assistant was packing.

The first was easy; a Batarang clipped him in the throat. The gun tumbled from his hands. He fell to his hands and knees and started gasping for air. He'd recover, but swallowing would hurt for the next week.

The second opened fire. The wall behind my head exploded into dust.

The third one surprised me.

He nailed me like a high school linebacker—which he probably was, a couple of years ago—and pushed me right back out the open window.

Out.

And.

Down.

I fell, free and clear.

Pavement rushed up to meet me.

I reached out for the Batrope hanging along the side of the building.

Missed it.

Déjà vu, Batman.

*No more Bruce* . . . I heard my father's voice.

But this time I had a second Batrope attached to my utility belt. I unsnapped it and looked up at the shattered window.

I saw the linebacker of a guard staring out of the opening, watching me plummet to my death.

I whipped the Batrope straight up with as much strength as my upper body would allow. The metal grappling hook at the end did its job—it made a loop around the arms and torso of the linebacker guard.

The line tightened.

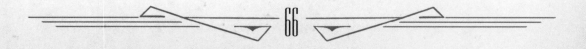

He screamed.

And now my life depended on how much this guy wanted to live. If he was smart, he'd throw his arms out to both sides and anchor his hands firmly against the metal frame of the window, even though 210 pounds of man was trying to pull him out and down, down, down. For him, giving up meant death.

He didn't want to die. He was smart. He held on.

I climbed up as fast as I could—which wasn't very fast at all. It probably seemed even longer to the linebacker.

When I made it back to the window, I didn't have to hurt the guard; he was already weak from the exertion. The man staggered back a few steps, knocked into a metal filing cabinet, and then fell down hard on his ass.

"Thanks for the lift," I told him.

"Batman!" the third guard cried. He seemed truly shocked. "I thought you were different. You're nothing but a common thief!"

He was pointing a gun at me.

I could see it trembling.

"I'm here for what's mine," I said. I used another Batarang to knock the pistol out of his hands, then a punch to knock him unconscious. I tried to hold back a little. The man seemed decent enough. I'd probably think the same thing about me, if I were in his $11-an-hour shoes.

Finally I raided Roman's vault. It was a TRTL 60x6 rated high-security safe—supposedly able to resist tools and torches on all six sides for at least sixty minutes. I was inside in twenty seconds. (I study the trade journals in my spare time.)

Inside the vault I found it: the missing page from my father's journal.

And every suspicion was confirmed.

I prey on the predators.

I am my father's son.

But I am also a detective.

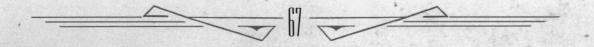

INSIDE THE VAULT I FOUND IT: THE MISSING
PAGE FROM MY FATHER'S JOURNAL.

THANK YOU

ACCESSING BAT COMPUTER FILES

> > STANDBY < <

# THE SOLUTION

Everybody who wears a Gotham City PD badge working homicide knows that you either solve a whodunnit within the first twenty-four hours . . . or you don't solve it at all. Fiona Scott's homicide was close to thirty years old, and it would have probably remained unsolved had it not been for one man who was determined to bring shame to the Wayne Family name.

In this case, the who was easy—as it usually is.

The problem: There was more than one *who*.

And the key to solving Fiona Scott's death was linking all of the whos together.

The first who, of course, was Roman Sionis. I had my suspicions when I first set foot on the *Aubrey James* to meet him for that drink. There was something about the way he held his right hand in his jacket, unwilling to remove it, even when I asked him to write something down. His note on the cocktail napkin was clearly written the opposite hand from the one to which he's accustomed. Roman was hiding something: the broken finger he'd received in Crime Alley.

Beyond that, the writing on that cocktail napkin was strikingly similar to the handwriting on the back of the party invitation found with Fiona Scott's body. I'm not a professional graphologist, but even a hobbyist could see the similarities between the two sets of letters. That's why I asked him to print rather than write in cursive. It made the comparison easier.

Roman wrote both.

The address in the note was just as damning. Roman sent me to visit his family's ex-butler, Ethan Abbott, who had been fully prepped for my arrival. I took a chance. I told him I was one of Roman's attorneys, and I'd been sent to hear his story—just another trial run.

"Pretend I'm Bruce Wayne," I told him. "He's here, right now, in front of you. And he asks you: What do you remember about Fiona Scott?"

Oh yes, he'd said. I remember everything. In perfect detail. You'll see.

I baited him: "You do."

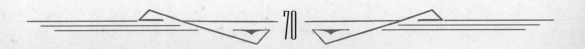

By now he was in full character, delivering the story as planned:

"Of COURSE I do! Just because you find me here in this pit of despair does not mean my faculties have entirely departed, sir!"

At the end, even Ethan Abbott asked how he'd done. When I saw his meager belongings gathered up in boxes, and his name missing from the nameplate holder outside, I realized what Roman had promised him: a better room somewhere else in Gotham.

And Roman had steered me right to him.

I was supposed to have introduced myself as Bruce Wayne and heard the shocking details of how my parents had allegedly killed Fiona Scott in cold blood and then covered up her murder as quickly as possible. A story he'd no doubt repeat to the Gotham PD when the time came.

But as I listened to the details, I realized something just as horrifying.

I was listening to the real events of the murder. Except the perpetrators were not my parent's but Roman's—Fredric and Dorothy.

I flashed back to the party photo Alfred showed me. I'll admit, I was distracted by the sight of my father in a bat mask. But when I saw Roman's mother wearing a silver mask—just like the one one the skeleton of Fiona Scott—I knew it was too strange to be a coincidence.

It wasn't something a professional killer would do. Too sloppy.

It was, however, an act of jealous spite. A final insult to grievous injury.

What could have sparked such rage?

The answer was in the letter to my father from the Gotham Clinic.

*The baby.*

When I first read that letter, I had felt my heart momentarily sink into a deep pit—deeper than I'd ever known. Deeper than even my parents' murder, because until that moment, their deaths were innocent. My parents' blood was clean. The note, however, presented a nightmare come to life. For a few awful moments, my father was not the man I remembered him to be. He was a monster.

That, together with the page from his journal, temporarily damned him in my eyes. He had carried on an affair with Fiona Scott. She had been pregnant with his child. And he had hidden

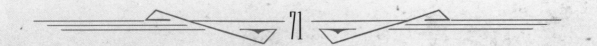

her away in a private clinic until the baby was born, only to reject her and, ultimately, murder her not long after . . .

Until I stepped back from the situation and looked at it like a detective.

Who was the nurturer?

And who was the philanderer?

My father was true.

The baby's father was Fredric Sionis.

Fredric had a burning need to compete with my father—and he wanted to prove he could possess anyone, including my father's beautiful secretary . . . who, Sionis assumed, was having an affair with my father. (Fredric, as mentioned in the *Gotham Globe* article, was a womanizer of epic proportions.)

The page of my father's journal mentions a reference to "going to see Fredric." Upon first reading these words, I had assumed it was an unrelated note. But it was very much related.

That's why I played on a hunch and broke into Roman's office vault to see if he had the missing journal page.

He did.

For Roman, that page had been easy enough to locate and steal; sadly, the Gotham University Library lacks the security measures of the Batcave.

And that missing page had given Roman everything he needed. And told me everything I needed to know.

According to my father's journal, he had learned of Fiona's "trouble" with Fredric Sionis and offered to pay for every medical expense to ensure her baby was born healthy. It didn't matter who the father was, or the circumstances; she was a young woman who needed help. And, sworn to do no harm, Thomas Wayne gave her what she needed.

What happened next—after the baby was born and Fiona returned to Wayne Enterprises—became clear when I read the missing page.

Fiona Scott was still very much depressed that Fredric refused to acknowledge the baby as his son. She didn't want his money and was willing to sign legal documents to that effect. But

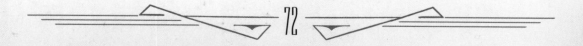

Fredric told her: "I already have a son."

At the costume party, she told my father that although she appreciated his kindness, she was moving in with her mother in Houston, Texas. But what my father didn't know was that Fiona went to the Sionis house one last time, desperate to convince Fredric to do the right thing—to be involved in their baby boy's life.

When Dorothy found her husband and Fiona talking on their patio, and overhead their conversation, she attacked Fiona with the wrought-iron flower holder.

And killed her.

In exactly the manner that their manservant, Ethan Abbott, reported.

Fredric and Dorothy then covered up the crime by wrapping Fiona in a tarp and burying her in a vault in the Sionis family mausoleum. They didn't even bother to remove her jade neck-

lace—the one Alfred recognized.

The necklace helped me unravel the sequence of events leading up to the discovery of the body buried in my front lawn. At every turn, Roman imitated what had happened in his own family, trying to make it look as if it had happened to the Wayne family.

Ethan Abbott had a story about a grisly murder and cover-up, perpetrated by Dr. Thomas and Martha Wayne.

In reality, Fredric and Dorothy Sionis had committed the crimes.

My family's mausoleum had been vandalized and made to look as if a body had been stored and then broken out for reburial.

I can only assume that a visit to the Sionis family mausoleum will reveal evidence of Fiona Scott's body having once been there, decomposing, for much of the past thirty years.

But why the removal of the body? This part was Roman being clever. He found out about the work under way on the grounds of Wayne Manor. It's not as though it was a huge secret—the construction crews had been working steadily for quite a while.

What better revenge than to have Bruce Wayne discover that his parents had killed a poor innocent girl and then tried to cover the evidence by burying her in the front lawn of Wayne Manor. There she would lie untouched for centuries, unlike the family vault, which would be opened in the event of Bruce Wayne's death. But how did Roman move the body and rebury it on the grounds?

Easy.

Inside help.

Inside his thug's wallet was a detailed map of the Wayne estate. That meant someone on the construction crew was feeding Roman information. Someone who might even do the dirty work for him.

The problem of course, was another *who*.

Who could Roman pay to take part in framing someone for murder? This wasn't just an odd job for a hatchet man or legbreaker. This was deep.

It nagged at me.

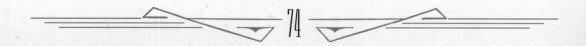

But when I heard the news that a construction worker had been killed at Wayne Manor, it all started to click. I felt the twitch in my gut, trying to force my brain to make a connection.

By the time Roman had been unmasked, I had a wild theory I needed to play out.

I asked Gordon for that blood test because I had a feeling Roman and the murder victim, Matthew Foster, were connected.

By blood.

And the test confirmed it: Fredric Sionis was their father.

All this information was enough to convince Gordon to raid Roman's office, send a forensics team to the Sionis family mausoleum, and bring in Ethan Abbott—the only material witness to this cold case—for questioning.

And over the past few days of police investigation, along with Abbott's testimony and Roman Sinonis's confession, the complete story has come to light.

A bitter, ugly light.

Fiona Scott had a baby boy at the Gotham Clinic. She took him home to her mother in Houston, and then she returned to work at Wayne Enterprises—just to wrap up loose ends, her relatives told Gordon.

She never came back.

Fiona's mother assumed she wanted to start over somewhere fresh. She didn't begrudge her daughter that. She saw how much the trauma had torn her apart.

She vowed to raise the boy on her own.

But Fiona's son grew up and eventually became curious about his parents. He knew his mother had disappeared when he was just a few months old, leaving him in his grandmother's care.

And his father—according to the boy's grandmother—was someone big and important. But she had refused to tell him who until she was on her deathbed. And that's how he discovered that he was the heir to the Sionis family fortune.

As she lay dying, his grandmother had whispered the name: "Fredric Sionis."

At first, Fiona's son confronted Roman himself, trying to force him into sharing his fortune. Roman's first urge was to have this threat destroyed. But then he saw a use for him, a way to use

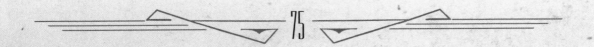

his newly discovered half-brother to shame the Wayne family.

That was when Roman told his half-brother that his mother hadn't disappeared. She had been murdered.

"Dr. Thomas Wayne did it," Roman had said.

A plan was hatched.

A plan for vengeance.

How do you get close enough to Wayne Manor to strangle it?

It's easy when you join the construction crew under the name Matthew Foster.

It was Foster who deposited his own mother's dead body and waited for it to be discovered. Meanwhile, Roman Sionis called the *Gotham Globe* with a tip and later sent incriminating documents—including the letter from the Gotham Clinic—to Jim Gordon.

And he taunted me along the way, wearing his hideous mask.

A mask that looked very much like the one Fredric Sionis wore the night of the masquerade ball.

Alfred discovered more photos. Fredric Sionis had worn a grotesque black mask that night—a warped version of the classic "tragedy" mask. His son Roman had remembered it.

The Gotham police found Roman's mother's diary among his possessions. He admitted to reading it not long ago and learning what his parents had done. Dorothy had spelled it out in great detail.

"They've paid," Roman told Gordon. "Oh, how they've paid." None of us know what he meant by that.

There is probably more investigating to do. What is clear is that Roman murdered his own half-brother just to tie up a loose end. There was no better way than to silence his co-conspirator and incriminate his nemesis, Bruce Wayne, in the process.

As I sit here and type this, I wonder about Roman. Did he always have this hatred and vengeance in him? Was it there, when he taunted me as a child and burned the faces from my toys, rendering them into pale, fleshy masks?

Most of all, I wonder what Roman sees when he looks in the mirror.

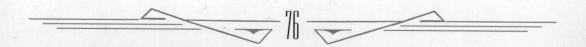

ROMAN'S BOUND FOR ARKHAM ASYLUM,
WHERE HE'LL UNDERGO THERAPY.

# THE ALLEY

I saw Roman Sionis off today. He didn't seem to notice I was in the crowd. Roman's bound for Arkham Asylum, where he'll undergo therapy. His lawyers got him off on an insanity plea. As he was led away on the perp walk, I resisted the urge to stick out my tongue at him.

On the way home, I stopped by the alley.

Years ago, I swore to avenge my parents' deaths by spending the rest of my life waging war against those who prey on the innocent.

Today, I swore to never again doubt my father. I knelt down and asked for forgiveness.

Prayed for it, actually.

After a long while, there was a voice behind me.

"Time to go, Master Bruce."

I think you hear me, don't you, Dad?

I have to imagine that you do.

## SPECIAL THANKS TO . . .

The teams at Quirk and DC Comics, especially my editor Jason Rekulak; our partner in Gotham crime, John Morgan; designer Doogie Horner; illustrator David Lapham; my wife, Meredith, for indulging my weekly comics runs for years now; Parker and Sarah, who will eventually benefit from my weekly comics runs (there's a lot of good reading ahead of you guys); every writer who's penned a Gotham City adventure, but I'd like to tip my hat to my favorites: Neal Adams, Ed Brubaker, Andy Diggle, Chuck Dixon, Joe R. Lansdale, Frank Miller, Grant Morrison, and Greg Rucka; and most especially Doug Moench, who introduced Black Mask to the pages of Batman along with artist Tom Mandrake; and, of course, Bob Kane and Bill Finger, for introducing the world to the Caped Crusader.